Silly Stories from

Here, There

and

Everywhere

Retold by Sean Taylor
Illustrated by Brett Hudson,
Nick Schon and Eric Smith

Contents

THE MAN WHO RODE A TIGER

A story from India

Once there was a tiger. It was big and fierce, as tigers are, but it was also rather stupid.

One dark night, a howling gale was blowing. Rain fell like spears, and thunder cracked like a whip above the clouds.

The tiger hated getting cold and wet, so it crept up to the wall of a small house where it could shelter. But then it heard an awful yelling from inside. A woman was shouting at the top of her voice. The roof of her house was full of holes, and the rain was coming in.

"Stop it! Stop it!" the woman screamed, as the water drip-drip-dripped through the roof. "Stop, you terrible drip, drip, drip!"

What can a 'terrible drip-drip-drip' be? thought the tiger. It must be a terrible creature.

At that moment, a little old farmer
came along. His donkey had run off in
the storm and he was searching for it.

"Where are you, you short-legged,
flea-bitten old nag?" he called out,
feeling his way in the dark. Then he
bumped into the tiger.

"Ah-ha!" he said, grabbing the tiger by the ear. "Now let's see you try to run off again." And he started to beat the tiger with a stick.

Well, the tiger did not know what was happening. "It must be the terrible drip-drip-drip!" it said. "Now it's got *me*. No wonder that woman was terrified!"

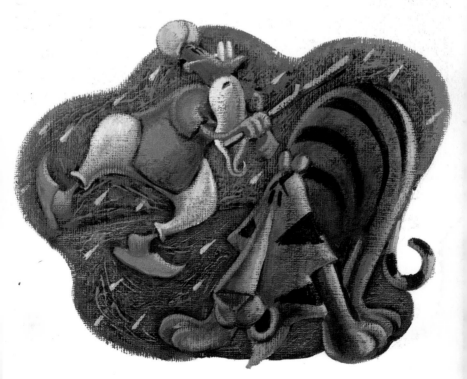

The next thing the tiger knew, the
farmer was tying a rope round its neck
and dragging it away from the house.
The tiger didn't even think of trying to
escape. And when the farmer climbed
onto its back, it quickly carried him
home. There, the farmer tied the tiger to
a post and went in to bed.

In the morning, the farmer's wife nearly jumped out of her skin when she saw the tiger outside her house.

"Do you know what you brought home last night?" she shouted to her husband.

"Just that lazy old donkey of mine," yawned the farmer.

"It's not your lazy old donkey!" said his wife.

"Of course it is," said the farmer, getting up to have a look. Then he saw the tiger.

"How did that tiger get there?" he asked.

"You must have brought it home," his wife said.

"I never did," said the farmer. "I rode home on my donkey."

"Well, your donkey's not there. So you must have ridden home on that tiger."

When the farmer realised what he had done, he shook like a leaf.

"We've got to get rid of it!" he said.

So his wife went out, cut the rope, and the tiger ran away.

News spread quickly about the man who rode a tiger. And the little old farmer enjoyed his sudden fame.

Soon, even the King came to hear about the farmer.

"Excellent!" he said. "A man who can ride a tiger is just what I need. Such a fearless man will easily see off my enemies!"

So he sent a messenger to ask the farmer for his help. The messenger also brought the King's largest war horse, because the King had said, "A man who can ride a tiger will need a great horse to ride upon."

When the farmer heard of the King's plan and saw the horse, he didn't know which way to turn.

"Look at this huge horse!" he said to his wife. "I don't even know how to get onto a thing like that. I'm used to a short-legged old donkey."

"You'll just have to jump," said his wife.

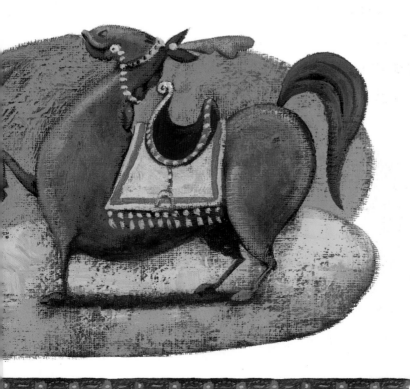

So the farmer jumped. First, he hit his head on the saddle. Then he got his beard tangled in the stirrups. Then he leapt with all his strength and landed on the horse's back. But he was facing the horse's tail instead of its head!

"Turn around!" called his wife.

"I can't," said the farmer. "I'll fall off!"

"Then I'll get a rope and tie you to the saddle the way you are," said his wife. And that is what she did.

The horse galloped away. The farmer didn't know where it was heading. And when he peeped over his shoulder, his face went pale. Directly ahead was a huge army of enemy soldiers.

"Stop!" shouted the farmer. But the horse didn't stop. The farmer grabbed at a tree to try to stop the horse. But the horse was going so fast that the tree came straight out of the ground!

The enemy soldiers stood in terror as the farmer came thundering towards them, waving a tree.

"Who is this man that can ride a horse backwards and that uses a tree as a spear?" they yelled. And with that, they ran for their lives and were never seen again.

When the King heard that his enemies
had been scattered, he was very pleased.
He said to the farmer, "I will send my
men to capture a tiger for you to ride!"

"Thank you, Sir," said the farmer.
"But riding a tiger is very easy for me
these days. What I would really like
is for someone to find my old donkey."

So the lost donkey was found. And
that is how the man who rode a
tiger ended up riding a short-legged,
flea-bitten old donkey.

The Princess and the Flea

A story from Brazil

Many years ago, there lived a princess.
The Princess was very beautiful, but she
was also very fussy. She would scream
at the top of her voice, and faint at least
three times a day.

One day, a maid was brushing the
Princess's hair, and said, "Oh! Princess!
Look what I've found in your hair.
A flea!" And she held out the flea on
her finger.

When the Princess saw the flea, she gave the loudest scream of her life and fainted. But she soon came round and demanded, "Let me see that flea again!"

The maid showed her the flea and the Princess said, "Actually it's rather cute and I'm going to keep it as a pet."

So the royal carpenter made a special box, and the flea was put inside it on a tiny cushion.

When the King heard about the flea, he was horrified. "Princess!" he said. "You can have a pet rabbit, a dog, a tiger, anything … but not a flea!"

But the Princess shook her head. "I'm the Princess and this is my pet!"

The Princess spoiled the flea and it grew bigger and bigger, until one day the King said, "Enough is enough! I am going to kill the flea and make a chair out of its skin. Then I will send an invitation to all the handsome princes in the world. If one of them can guess what the chair is made out of, he will receive your hand in marriage!"

Well, the Princess liked the sound of
handsome princes, so she agreed. The
flea was killed, the chair was made, and
within days, the princes began arriving
at the palace. But not one of them could
guess what the chair was made of.

"It's made from lizard's skin!"

"No."

"Might it be snake's skin?"

"No."

"Alligator's skin?"

"Certainly not."

A young lad called Chico heard about the chair. So he put on his straw hat and set off for the palace. On the way, he shared his lunch with an old blind man. In return, the man gave him a little piece of straw.

"Blow down this straw whenever you're in trouble," said the man.

The straw looked perfectly ordinary to Chico, but he put it in his pocket anyway.

When Chico walked into the palace, the King said, "Right, young man, tell me what this chair is made of."

Chico walked around the chair three times. But he couldn't tell what it was made of. Then he remembered the piece of straw that the old man had given him. Perhaps it's worth a try, he thought. So he put the straw in the corner of his mouth and blew softly down it.

At once, Chico knew what the chair was made of.

"This chair is made of ... FLEA SKIN!" he said.

The Princess fainted.

"Correct!" gasped the King.

"So do I marry the Princess now or later?" asked Chico.

The Princess came round. "I can't marry him," she whispered, fiddling with her pearl necklace. "He chews a piece of straw and wears a silly hat. Give him a harder test!"

So the King said, "For your second test you will be given ... one hundred parrots. You must take them into the rainforest and return at nightfall with all one hundred."

Chico went off with one hundred parrots. But as soon as he left the palace gates, the birds flew off in one hundred different directions! Chico took out the magic straw and blew down it. All the parrots came flying back.

When the Princess heard that Chico had not lost any of the parrots, she sent a maid into the rainforest to trick him.

The maid said to Chico, "I would like to buy one of your parrots."

Chico replied, "I won't sell, lend or borrow my parrots, but I will *give* you one … in return for ten kisses!"

The maid gave Chico ten kisses, five on each cheek. Then she hurried away with a parrot. But, before she reached the palace, Chico blew down the straw and the parrot flew back to him.

So the Princess sent a second maid into the rainforest. The second maid gave Chico twenty kisses – ten on each cheek. In return he gave her two parrots. But, before she reached the palace, Chico blew down the straw and the parrots flew back to him.

So the Princess put on a disguise and went into the rainforest herself. Chico recognised her at once.

"I would like to buy three of your parrots," she said.

Chico replied, "I won't sell, lend or borrow my parrots, but I will *give* you three in return for your pearl necklace!"

The Princess was furious, but she wanted to trick Chico into giving away the parrots. So she gave him her pearl necklace. Chico gave her three parrots. Then off she ran, back to the palace.

But, before the Princess reached the palace, Chico blew once again down the magic straw. The parrots flew back to him.

At nightfall, Chico returned to the palace. The King was amazed to see Chico with all one hundred parrots.

"Do I marry the Princess now or later?" Chico asked.

The Princess whispered to the King, "Give him one more test!"

The King said, "For your last test you will be given ... an empty bag. And you must fill it with lies!"

A large bag was handed to Chico. He said, "Your Majesty, did you know that in return for a parrot, this maid here gave me ten kisses?"

The maid was embarrassed. "No, I didn't!" she lied.

Chico opened the bag as if catching her words. Then he said, "And did you know that in return for two parrots, that maid there gave me twenty kisses?"

The maid was embarrassed. "No, I didn't!" she lied.

Chico opened the bag again.

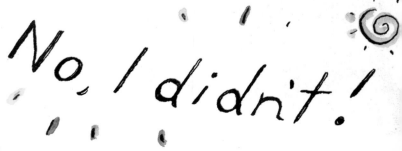

No, I didn't!

31

Then Chico looked at the Princess and said to the King, "Did you know that in return for three parrots, the Princess gave me her pearl necklace, and won my heart!"

"I most certainly did not," lied the Princess.

Chico opened the bag as if catching her words. Then he tied a string around it and said, "Your Majesty, this bag is full of lies!"

"It is," said the King, "and all that remains to be seen is whether the Princess wishes to marry you or not!"

Chico looked at the Princess and she looked at him. And, because he was braver, funnier and cleverer than all the handsome princes put together, she agreed.

THE KING OF TALL STORIES

A story from Ireland

Once there was a lad called Timmy.
Now Timmy was a good lad, but he had
one fault – he loved telling tall stories –
stories that are impossible to believe.

Once his mother sent him out to
gather firewood and he said he couldn't
find any because the woods had blown
away! Oh yes, Timmy loved to tell
tall stories.

One day his mother said to him, "Timmy, it's time you went out to seek your fortune. But don't tell any tall stories – they'll only get you into trouble."

"Mother," said Timmy, "I will go out to seek my fortune, and we'll see if telling tall stories gets me into trouble."

Timmy hadn't gone very far when he
spotted a poster nailed to a tree.
It read:

The King of Tall
Stories is holding a
Competition.
He will give a chest
full of gold to
anyone who can tell
him a tall story that
makes him shout out,
"THAT'S NOT TRUE!"

"Well," said Timmy, "if there's one thing
I'm good at, it's telling tall stories. So off
he went to the land of the King of Tall
Stories.

Eventually, Timmy arrived at the
castle of the King of Tall Stories.

"I suppose you're here for the
competition?" said the King.

"I am indeed," said Timmy.

"Good," said the King. "Come on in
and I'll show you around."

The King led Timmy into the kitchen, where a cook was cutting up a turnip as big as a football.

"I bet you've never seen a turnip that big before," said the King.

"I have indeed," answered Timmy. "Where I live, the turnips are enormous. Last year we grew one so big that a goat ate her way inside it. It took her a week to come out the other side. When she'd finished, there was space inside for a family with four children to move in."

"Is that so?" said the King with a twinkle in his eyes.

The King didn't believe a word of Timmy's tall story, but he didn't want Timmy to win the competition, so he didn't say anything.

Next, the King took Timmy into a courtyard, where there were twenty or more beehives.

"I bet you've never seen as many beehives as that," said the King.

"I have indeed," answered Timmy. "Where I come from, we have three hundred and sixty-five beehives. It's my job to count the bees when they go out in the morning and then again when they come back at night.

Once there was a bee missing at the end of the day. So I got onto an old donkey and went looking for it. I had a job finding it, but eventually I did. Do you know that bee had gathered so much nectar that it couldn't fly?

I cut some reeds, wove two baskets, and slung them over the donkey's back. Then I filled them with the nectar. It was so heavy that the donkey could hardly walk. I had to pick him up and carry him home on my head."

"Is that so?" said the King of Tall Stories.

The King didn't believe a word of Timmy's tall story, but he didn't want Timmy to win the competition, so he didn't say anything.

Next, Timmy was taken into a garden where there stood a very tall cherry tree.

"I bet you've never seen a cherry tree as tall as that," said the King.

"I have indeed," answered Timmy. "Where I come from, there is a cherry tree so tall that it goes right the way up to the sky.

Once I decided to climb up the tree
to pick some cherries. I climbed and
climbed and climbed, and would you
believe it, I reached heaven itself? So I
had a bit of a look around, but a terrible
storm started howling down below and
the cherry tree blew down."

"What did you do?" asked the King.

"Well," said Timmy, "I found some straw and twisted it into a rope. Then I tied the rope to the gates of heaven and started to let myself down. But the rope wasn't strong enough. It snapped, and I started to fall back down to Earth.

I had an apple in my pocket and I threw it down the chimney of our house. When my mother saw the apple coming down the chimney, she guessed something was wrong and she came rushing out of the house.

She held out her apron and, just in time, she caught me. But the apron was not strong enough to hold me. I fell straight through it and rolled down into the river.

At that very moment, a big fish was swimming by. I grabbed it and pulled it out of the water. I brought it into the kitchen and put it down on the kitchen table. My mother cut the fish open and inside there was a book.

In the book, we read, 'Once the King of Tall Stories was very poor. His father used to work for Timmy's father, peeling potatoes for sixpence a month.' "

The King was really angry. He didn't want people to think that his father was very poor. He couldn't stop himself and he burst out, "THAT'S NOT TRUE!"

"Ah-ha! Tricked you!" said Timmy. "Now where's that chest of gold?"

And that is how Timmy made his fortune. He's still rich to this day. The last time I saw him, he was using twenty-pound notes to light his fire!